our generation

This is Katelyn's story.

W9-APU-587

KATELYN ™

BLIZZARD ON MOOSE MOUNTAIN

BY

JULIE DRISCOLL

COVER ART BY KRISTI VALIANT
STORY ILLUSTRATIONS BY KELLY MURPHY

An Our Generation® *book*

MAISON JOSEPH BATTAT LTD *Publisher*

A very special thanks to the editor,
Joanne Burke Casey.

Our Generation®
Books is a registered trademark of Maison Joseph Battat Ltd.
Text copyright © 2007 by Julie Driscoll
Characters portrayed in this book are fictitious. Any references to historical
events, real people, or real locales are used fictitiously. Other names,
characters, places, and incidents are products of the author's imagination,
and any resemblance to actual events or locales or persons, living or dead,
is entirely coincidental.
All rights reserved, including the right of reproduction in whole or in part
in any form.
ISBN: 978-0-9794542-0-2
Printed in China

For Emily, Kerry and Steve.
Thanks for all your support
and inspiration.

Read all the adventures in the
Our Generation® Book Series

The Mystery of the Vanishing Coin
featuring Eva™

Adventures at Shelby Stables
featuring Lily Anna™

One Smart Cookie
featuring Hally™

Blizzard on Moose Mountain
featuring Katelyn™

Stars in Your Eyes
featuring Sydney Lee™

The Note in the Piano
featuring Mary Lyn™

Table of Contents

Chapter One	The Sticky Situation	**Page 9**
Chapter Two	Decisions, Decisions	**Page 17**
Chapter Three	Brake for Moose! Bear on the Loose!	**Page 24**
Chapter Four	What a Sap!	**Page 33**
Chapter Five	Snow, Snow Go Away & Don't Come Back—Ever!	**Page 41**
Chapter Six	Cabin Fever	**Page 46**
Chapter Seven	Slow Man	**Page 55**
Chapter Eight	I'll Moose You	**Page 60**
Chapter Nine	Nervous Nellies	**Page 65**
Chapter Ten	Still a Sticky Situation	**Page 79**
Chapter Eleven	Choosing to Choose	**Page 84**
Chapter Twelve	Don't Bug Me!	**Page 90**

EXTRA! EXTRA! READ ALL ABOUT IT!
*Big words, wacky words, powerful words, funny words…
what do they all mean?
Look for words with the symbol *. They're in the Glossary
with their meanings at the end of this book.*

Chapter One
THE STICKY SITUATION

Annie Hill's skates were old and worn. The white leather was spattered with brown scuff marks and the rust spots on the blades made it difficult to see any reflection at all. My skates were shiny and new.

Annie's leggings were faded and a little short. There was a small hole forming at the knee. My warm-up clothes were brand new and fit just right.

Annie had recently moved here with her mom, dad and two sisters. And even though her skates were old and her clothes were not very stylish, she was special to me and I liked her.

There was only one problem. My friends didn't like her. They didn't want her to be a part of our group and this, as my annoying little brother Bobby would say, made for a VERY STICKY SITUATION indeed!

It was school vacation week and also the week of my annual* ice skating competition*. My parents decided to take a short vacation before the competition. I really wanted to stay home and practice my toe loops* and backward crossovers* with Annie. Instead, there I was, riding in a car with my mom, dad and brother Bobby. We were headed up to a cabin on Moose Mountain. Oh joy!

Bobby is always coming up with a new obsession*. Last month it was frogs, before that it was tornadoes and this month it's silly little sayings like HOT DIGGITY DOG and GEEZ LOUISE. I mean really. Who the heck is Louise anyway? I had to hum and block my ears for most of the ride.

I had a lot of time to think during the long car ride so I thought about the competition. I had been practicing so hard. I hoped that I would get a medal this time. I had been competing for three years, trying my absolute hardest to get my routine just right—but no medal yet.

I mostly thought about Annie, though. I remembered how I had hurt Annie's feelings and I wondered what she was doing that minute. Was she sad? Did she hate me? I hoped not.

I thought about the first time that my friends, Caroline, Casey, Sarah, and I noticed Annie. We were in the school cafeteria, sitting at our special table.

The four of us have been friends since kindergarten and we've been sitting at our special table since as long as I can remember. Being friends for so long, we've been through a lot together. And the one thing that I've learned is that we are all far from perfect.

For instance, Caroline is a little bossy. Whatever she says, goes. But she would do anything for us. She's always bringing us gifts, inviting us for sleepover parties and making us feel special.

Casey is just plain fun. She's bubbly and *extremely* talkative. She talks and talks and talks. Sometimes, after listening to her, I feel like I need to take a nap. She chews her gum really loud and that kind of bugs me. And she goes along with whatever Caroline says because it's just easier that way.

Then there is Sarah. I don't know how else to describe Sarah except to say that I'm not sure if she has a lot going on upstairs—if you get my drift. She is nice. She is a little shy. But that's not why I think that she's not very smart. It's mainly because she can't seem to make any decisions about anything on her own.

If Caroline says that the boy who sits in front of her is bad news then, to Sarah, he is bad news. And she will tell everyone else that *that* boy is bad news, even if he isn't.

If Caroline thinks that blue is the best color in the world and no other color is better, well then, blue it is! Sarah will wear blue, talk about blue and adopt the notion* that she really loves blue to the point that everyone thinks that Sarah is the one who came up with the idea herself.

As for me, well, I guess I'm a mixture of all of them. I have strong opinions just like Caroline. When I disagree with her things are a little awkward* for a few days. I'm a little bubbly, but not as much as Casey. And sometimes I can even be shy, like Sarah.

But despite all of our quirks*, we are friends. I always feel safe when I'm with my friends. I always feel as if I can be myself and not be judged for it. And I guess that's what friendship is all about.

Anyhow, we were sitting at our special table when we noticed Annie standing in the lunch line.

"That's the new girl," said Casey.

I glanced over at Annie. She was wearing a pair of light blue overalls and a red plaid shirt. Her straight black hair rested on her shoulders

and her eyes were big and dark. I thought she looked like a beautiful princess who was wearing grungy* clothes to disguise her identity.

"She's in Mrs. Doyle's class with me," said Sarah. "She moved here from Minnesota. Her dad is a farmer or something and someone said she has a porcupine for a pet."

"OK, well, that's a little weird," said Caroline.

"That has to be a mistake. We should ask her to sit with us and find out," I said.

"I don't think so," protested Caroline. "Farmers aren't my type. Besides, I like our group just the way it is." And as usual, Casey and Sarah agreed with Caroline.

"I think that she's pretty and she sounds interesting," I said, as I watched Annie walk over to a table and sit down by herself.

Eventually, kids began filling in the seats around her. Not because they wanted to sit with her, but because there was no place else to sit.

That was at the beginning of the year.

And I remember thinking to myself that Annie would probably meet some nice new friends in Mrs. Doyle's class and that it wasn't my responsibility to help her.

It's funny how circumstances* in life take you down a path you weren't expecting to travel on. That's what happened with Annie and me.

Chapter Two
DECISIONS, DECISIONS

Shortly after the school year began, I started my skating lessons. I had been practicing with Mrs. Billings, my skating coach, for six years. As fate* would have it, Annie was also a skater, and her lesson was just before mine.

In the beginning, when Annie's lesson was ending, we would simply smile as we passed one another on the ice. Soon after, we began saying hello.

Some days, Mrs. Billings would take a small break in between our lessons to talk to Annie's mom, or my mom, about our costumes or the skating competition that we were preparing for. Annie and I used that time to practice our spins and axels* together.

Before we knew it, we were meeting each other at the rink on weekends. Afterward, we would go over to Fred's Donut Shop for hot chocolate. That's where we came up with all of our secret friendship codes.

My brother Bobby called Annie my secret friend. Not because we had secret codes but because my other friends still didn't want to be friends with her. I hadn't necessarily been keeping my friendship with Annie a secret from Caroline, Casey and Sarah, but they sure were making it difficult for me.

It was most awkward during school lunch and recess. At lunchtime, Annie usually sat with some of the girls from her class. During recess I would sometimes try and sneak away to hang out with Annie. If Caroline, Casey or Sarah noticed then they would pretty much snub me for the rest of recess and for the rest of the day.

18

It was the day before we left for our trip. I was at the skating rink, waiting for my lesson to begin. I watched Annie out on the ice with Mrs. Billings. She looked so graceful as she glided across the ice, just like a ballerina on skates.

Annie looked over at me and smiled. She tapped her chin twice with her index finger. That was our secret code for *help me*. I pulled on my ear lobe. That meant I understood.

When Annie's lesson ended, Mrs. Billings wanted to show us our costumes. They had arrived a few days earlier. Our moms were excited to see them as well, and Bobby was hanging around just because he liked to be nosy.

I lifted my costume out of the box. It was light purple, like lilacs, with sparkly sleeves and a shimmery skirt. I really wanted the glittery red costume that I saw in the catalog but Mrs. Billings said that it would clash* with my winter wonderland routine.

"It's beautiful!" exclaimed Annie. My

mom agreed.

"Yeah," I said. "I guess so." But what I was really thinking was, *yeah but it isn't the glittery red costume and is simply another reminder of the many decisions that I am not allowed to make for myself.*

Annie reached into the box and pulled out her costume. Annie's mom looked pleased. "It will go perfectly with your routine," she said.

It was a velvety soft, white costume with a headband to match. Annie was going to be skating to one of my favorite songs, "Somewhere Over the Rainbow."

"I think it will look beautiful on you," I said to Annie. Annie smiled.

"Should I wear my hair in braids or a bun, Katelyn?" she asked.

"Definitely braids," I answered. "I'm going to wear a high ponytail."

"A bun," interrupted Mrs. Billings. "I want you both to wear your hair in a bun!"

I began to feel the frustration building up

inside of me. When would I ever get to make a decision for myself? Why did we have to take a vacation before my competition? I really needed the extra time to practice. Why couldn't I wear the red costume? Why not a ponytail? Why, why, why?

"Do you want to come over tonight and practice doing hair and makeup since you're leaving tomorrow?" Annie asked, snapping me out of my anger.

Annie had never invited me over to her house before. But I knew I couldn't go and I didn't want to tell her why. "I can't. I have to get ready for our trip," I fibbed*, not wanting to hurt her feelings.

"No, Katelyn," said Bobby, "you're going to that pizza party tonight, remember?"

Caroline was having a "beginning of the vacation" pizza party. Many of the kids from our class and Sarah's and Annie's class were invited, but not Annie.

And there it was, the hurtful truth, out in

the open! My heart sank. I could see the disappointment in Annie's face even though she was trying hard not to show it.

"Oh yeah, that's right," I said, playing dumb.

"That's OK," said Annie, "we can do it some other time."

Then it was time for my lesson. I said goodbye to Annie and I told her that I would see her at the competition. I could tell that she was sad. I was sad, too.

And that's how I hurt Annie. That was the sticky situation that I was in—the sticky situation that seemed to be getting stickier and stickier by the minute.

Chapter Three
BRAKE FOR MOOSE!
BEAR ON THE LOOSE!

As we made our way further and further up into the mountains, my ears began to pop. My mom gave Bobby and me some chewing gum. She said that it would help.

Bobby sounded just like Casey when he chewed his gum. I couldn't decide whether I would prefer to listen to him rattle on and on about how ROOTIN' TOOTIN' happy he was to be going on a vacation or if I would rather have him sit there quietly, making loud chomping noises with his gum.

We were driving on a steep and winding road. I noticed that there were a lot of "Brake for Moose" signs. "What's with all the moose signs?" I asked my dad.

Dad began telling us a long and *boring* story about how there were a lot of car accidents involving moose. He said that we were in moose country and that...blah, blah, blah. My mind began to tune him out.

"Big moose!" yelled Bobby.

I figured that he was starting up again with more of his ridiculous* sayings so I ignored him. Apparently, so did Mom and Dad.

"GINORMOUS* moose!" shouted Bobby again. This time he was noticeably louder.

I looked up and, to my surprise, there was a gigantic moose strutting* slowly across the road. Mom yelled. The brakes screeched. The moose stopped in the middle of the road and stared at us sideways. He moved his mouth from side to side. It seemed as if he was telling Dad to slow down.

"He just mooed," said Bobby.

"Moose don't moo," I said. "He made more of an IEEE sound."

"No," said Bobby. "That moose mooed!"

I rolled my eyes. It wasn't worth arguing about.

Dad took out his camera and snapped a picture. The flash from the camera startled the moose. He trotted quickly across the road and disappeared into the woods.

"And as I was saying," Dad continued, "that's why there are so many 'Brake for Moose' signs."

We were almost to the cabin. Bobby and I

were beginning to get restless. Bobby reached into his backpack and pulled out a bag of waffles.

"What are you doing?" I asked, giving him a strange look.

"This is my waffle stash," he answered matter-of-factly. "I like waffles and I heard they sell a lot of maple syrup up here, so I brought a stash. You have a problem with that?"

"Whatever," I said. "Anything to keep you quiet."

Soon after, we came to a fork in the road. Dad wasn't sure which way to go. There was a small general store, just before the fork. We pulled over into the parking lot and Dad took out a map.

"What is that old saying?" asked my dad, as he examined the map. "Something like: If there is only one road then you don't get lost."

"If there is only one road then you also don't have to choose," my mother added.

"I have a saying," I said. "If you're a kid you never get to choose anyway, so who cares!"

27

My mother looked back at me with a "what is that supposed to mean?" look on her face.

"Bear," said Bobby.

I sighed. "Here we go again."

Mom and Dad were busy looking at the map.

"Bear," said Bobby again.

"Stop it, Bobby," said my mother.

I looked around. "I don't see any bear," I said.

"There is a bear up there!" he exclaimed, and he pointed to the tree across the street.

"Hey!" I yelled. "Look at the cute little bear up in the tree."

"Well, I'll be darned," said my dad. He grabbed his camera, jumped out of the car and started across the street.

All of a sudden a man came out of the store and hollered to my dad. We all got out of the car to see what was going on.

The man's name was Dave. He was the

owner of the general store. He was a tall, elderly looking man with a white beard. His gray hair was pulled back into a ponytail.

"HOWDY DOODY to you folks!" said Dave.

Bobby liked him right away.

Dave told us that the bear's name was Nellie. "Nellie comes by once in a while and

climbs that tree. But, that usually means her mother is nearby. If you get too close you might upset the mother and you don't want to do that."

"NO WAY JOSÉ!" agreed Bobby.

We decided to go into the general store and have a look around. There was a big sign on the door that read "If we don't have it, then you don't really need it." There were all sorts of interesting things to look at inside and it smelled really nice, like a mixture of old wood and new candles.

There were books, jams, maple syrup in fancy glass bottles and jugs, little gadgets and trinkets, lanterns, baskets, old metal tins, candy, postcards, little rag dolls and much more. Bobby and I could have stayed in there all day.

My eyes fixated* on an old pair of ice skates hanging on the wall. They reminded me of Annie's skates except they were even older and rustier. "Are you selling those ice skates?" I asked Dave.

"No," he said, "They're just for decoration."

"What are those?" I asked pointing to a pair of flat woven things that hung beside them. They reminded me of tennis rackets without the handles.

"Those are snowshoes," answered Dave. "They belonged to a beautiful young girl. Those were her skates, too. I hang them there for decoration and for memories."

∙❧ ❧∙

Dave gave my dad directions to our cabin. It was a short drive up the road.

Our mom let Bobby and me choose a few pieces of candy before we left. I chose my favorite, chocolate-covered turtles with caramel and cashews. Bobby chose sour gummy worms. Yuck!

We walked out of the store. Nellie was gone. I wondered where she had wandered off to.

Chapter Four
WHAT A SAP!

The cabin we were staying in was the coolest. It reminded me of my brother's Lincoln Logs® and the "Little House on the Prairie" house all rolled into one.

The living area was inviting with its large stone fireplace and walls made of timber*. An old wooden rocking chair stood on one side of the fireplace and a comfy looking chair on the other. A big sturdy* couch was positioned directly across from the fireplace and there was a braided rug on the floor. On the walls hung a pair of old snowshoes, metal tins and some baskets.

There was a small kitchen and an eating area. Over the dining table hung a chandelier* that looked like it was made out of moose antlers. A narrow wooden stairway led to the bedrooms on the second floor.

We ran up the stairs. Our bedroom was on the left. It had two double beds that looked so very warm and cozy with their colorful quilts and big fluffy pillows.

I didn't mind that I had to share a room with Bobby because I didn't particularly like being by myself in a strange new place.

"It's a real old-fashioned log cabin," I said.

"Yeah," said Bobby. "Get ready to HUN-KER down, 'cause we're gonna be roughing it I tell ya!"

I looked around. It didn't look rough to me. "Uh, Bobby," I said, "we have running water, electricity and heat."

"Well…" Bobby paused for a moment. "We better get going soon. Gotta get out and catch our dinner. I saw a stream. Maybe they have fish!"

"I don't think so," I replied. "Mom brought food."

"Can we at least put sleeping bags on the beds?" Bobby whined*.

"Oh brother!"

That night my mom made a nice dinner. Afterward we sat by the fire and played check-ers and charades. Then my mom told Bobby and me that it was time for bed. We climbed

into our warm, comfy beds and fell fast asleep.

❧ ❧

The next day, we went maple syruping. We arrived at an old farmhouse that was set up on the top of a mountain. The views from the farmhouse were incredible.

We could see all the other mountains at a distance and even the treetops. We were up so high I felt as if we were on top of the world.

We went inside. A woman came out from the back room to greet us. Her name was Bess. She was a short, round woman who waddled when she walked, sort of like a duck. It was as if her knees had no bend to them whatsoever.

Bess wore a red coat that had black round splotches on it. Bobby commented that she looked like a giant ladybug.

The maple syrup lady—as we came to call her—gave us a tour of the farm and showed us how to make maple syrup. We hiked into the woods, slowly, because the syrup lady wasn't very fast on her feet. I wanted to show her how to bend her knees, so that she could walk faster, but I didn't feel it was my place to do so.

She told us to select a sugar maple tree to tap. Tapping a tree meant that we were going to drill a hole into it to get the sap out. The maple syrup lady explained that the tree had to be at least ten inches in diameter*. She said that we didn't want to tap the smaller trees because they still needed the sap to help them grow.

"Here's one," said Bobby. Bobby selected a big tree. "What a SAP!" he joked. "Get it, SAP?"

"Yeah, Bobby," smiled Mom, "we get it."

The syrup lady showed us how to drill a hole into the tree. Then, she took a hammer, and hammered a spout into the hole.

We hung a bucket on the spout. Soon, sap began dripping into the bucket. Slowly, drip, drip, ping, ping, ping, into the pail. It was a clear, watery liquid.

"You picked a good tree," said Bess. "Taste it if you want."

Bobby and I placed our fingers under the dripping sap and tasted it. It had a slightly sweet taste.

There were a few buckets hanging on some of the other trees that were almost filled to the top with sap. We helped Bess empty the buckets into a gathering tank that sat on the back of a tractor. Then the tractor hauled* all of the sap back to a small building that was set behind the farmhouse. As we walked toward it, Bess explained, "This is the sugarhouse, where they boil down the sap and make it into maple syrup."

Steam was rising from the roof above the sugarhouse. We entered. It was very steamy inside and there was a strong, but pleasant maple smell. A man was standing at the boiling tank. He described, in detail, how the water from the sap eventually evaporated* and the thick sticky stuff that was left was real maple syrup. Then, he offered us samples.

He dipped a ladle into the big vat* of syrup and then poured the syrup into some small cups. I drank mine right away.

Bobby pulled a waffle from his coat pocket. He drizzled the syrup onto the waffle and took a bite. "MAPLE-ICIOUS!" he exclaimed. "Make sure you buy a lot of syrup before we leave here, Mom, 'cause I have a lot of waffles to eat!"

Later that day, after dinner, my mom and dad took Bobby and me to an ice skating park. It was all lit up and there were pretty decorations on the trees and fence surrounding the pond.

I was happy that I was able to practice my routine. I spun, jumped, twirled and just skated, round and round the pond. I felt free and light as a feather. *This vacation wasn't so bad after all,* I thought to myself. All of the problems back home didn't seem as important to me now. We were leaving in the morning for the skating competition. I couldn't wait to get there and see Annie. I just knew that everything was going to be OK.

❧ ❧

As I was practicing my layback spin*, I felt a snowflake touch my cheek. I looked up at the sky.

Little did I know—the tiny snowflake that touched my cheek was the beginning of a *huge* disaster!

Chapter Five

SNOW, SNOW GO AWAY & DON'T COME BACK—EVER!

The next morning I awoke to the sound of howling wind and rattling windows. I looked outside. Snow was swooshing and swirling about outside the cabin.

The ground was covered in white. I couldn't even see the trees that were only a few steps from the cabin. It was a full-blown blizzard!

I hurried downstairs. My dad was listening to the radio and my mom was cooking breakfast.

Bobby was running around the cabin like a crazy person, shouting, "This is SNOW much fun!"

I sat down at the kitchen table. My mom placed a plate of pancakes in front of me.

"We have some bad news Katelyn," she said. "The area has been hit hard with a nor'easter* and the roads are all closed. I'm sorry to have to tell you this, but we are not going to be able to make it to your skating competition."

I thought she was joking at first. "Can't we leave a little later today, after the snow stops?" I asked.

"I'm afraid not," said my dad. "The roads aren't plowed and they probably won't be for a few days."

"A few days!" I shouted. "What? This can't be happening. What about the competition?" I asked. "What will happen if I miss it?"

"There's nothing we can do," said my mom. "It's not safe to drive."

"Call Mrs. Billings. Tell her what happened," I said. "Maybe she can come get me or something."

"The phone lines are out," said my dad.

"What about your cell phone?" I asked in desperation.

"It doesn't work up here in the mountains," he answered. "Besides, no one would be crazy enough to try and drive up here in these conditions."

"Great! Just great!" I shouted.

"No," said Bobby. "You mean GRRRREAT! Like a bear, get it?" I told him to be quiet.

"Katelyn," Bobby continued, "even though you're a little grumpy, I still love you SNOW much. I like it here and I'm glad were staying. I'm SNOW very glad!" He smiled.

I didn't feel much like eating. My stomach was all in knots. I couldn't believe that this was happening to me.

For the entire morning I sat by the window and watched the snow coming down. There I was, stuck in a cabin in the woods with my crazy little brother who was now walking around the cabin with a pair of snowshoes on his feet and a tin pail on his head.

I thought about Annie. She was probably

already there by now, going over her routine and wondering where I was. I thought about all my hard work, all the practicing to get my routine just right. It seemed like such a waste of time. I stared out the window and began to cry.

Suddenly, there was a knock at the door. *Who*, I wondered, *could be out in such terrible weather?*

Chapter Six
CABIN FEVER

My dad opened the front door of the cabin. There was a man standing there with a pile of wood in his arms. Icicles were frozen to his beard and he was covered in snow from head to toe, like Mr. Jack Frost himself!

I wasn't sure, but I thought he kind of looked like Dave from the general store.

"HOWDY DOODY FOLKS!" he said.

Yeah, it was Dave all right!

"I thought you might need more wood and some food seeing as how you're probably going to be staying a while longer."

I sighed at the thought.

"Snowmobiles come in handy this time of year. I just hitch the trailer onto the back and I

can go just about anywhere."

My mom and dad were grateful to Dave for all his help. Dad helped Dave carry in the rest of the wood and the food. Dave's wife had sent over some bread and muffins that she made from scratch. Mom invited him to stay for some hot apple cider.

Bobby was excited to see Dave and show him how well he could walk in the snowshoes. "My mom says I'm suffering from cabin fever, but I don't feel sick," said Bobby.

Dave noticed me sitting over by the window. "What's with the long face?" he asked.

I still wasn't in the mood to speak so my mom answered for me. "We were supposed to leave today for her ice skating competition," she told Dave. "She's been looking forward to it all year."

"Not a happy camper," added Bobby, "NO SIRREE."

"Ahh," said Dave. "Well, I have just the cure for cabin fever and unhappy campers."

He reached into his coat pocket and pulled out a cloth sack. My mom took his coat and hat and hung them on a hook near the door. Dave walked over to the living area and plopped down on the big comfy chair near the fireplace.

Bobby and I were a little curious to see what was in the sack. We walked over and sat down on the rug. Dave emptied out the contents of the sack onto the rug. There were small strings, shiny needles and a bag containing tiny little beads of various colors.

"Have you ever heard of a friendship bracelet?" asked Dave.

I nodded.

"Beading is an old Abenaki tradition. These particular bracelets are popular today. Each of the different colored beads has a unique meaning and the pattern that you choose also has a meaning."

Dave placed the cloth sack on the rug and emptied some of the beads onto it. Then he

showed us how to poke at the little beads and scoop them up with a needle.

We pulled the needle and thread through seven beads. Then we wrapped the string of beads around our fingers to form a loop. We looped back through the first bead and then added another bead to make a little daisy.

"Is this a girl thing?" Bobby asked.

"No," replied Dave. "Boys make these bracelets too. If you replace the white beads on each side with a different color you can create tiny arrows instead of daisies."

"So who are the Abenakis anyways and how do you know so much about them?" asked Bobby as he poked at the tiny beads.

"The Abenakis are people, just like you and me. Some people refer to them as Native Americans but they just like to be called Abenakis," said Dave.

"The Abenakis were the first people to come and live in these parts. During the long, cold winters, the Abenaki children would pass the time by practicing the traditional* beading."

Mom brought over the apple cider.

"CINNALICIOUS!" exclaimed Bobby as he took a sip from his mug.

I still felt sad, but working on the bracelets gave me something to do.

"You know," Dave said to me, "you remind me a lot of a young Abenaki girl I once knew. Her name was Nina. Nina had a great love for the outdoors. Every chance she got, she would go out and just walk. She walked everywhere. In the wintertime she didn't let the snow stop her from doing what she loved to do. She simply strapped on her snowshoes and off she went."

He smiled. "She also loved to ice skate. She was a very good ice skater. But, mostly, she just liked to walk. When the wind was howling, like it is today, and Nina was forced to stay inside, she was not happy."

"Not a happy camper," added Bobby.

"NO SIRREE," smiled Dave.

"One day, when Nina was stuck inside, Nina's mom taught her how to make these bracelets. Eventually, she found that being still was not such a bad thing. Using your hands to make beautiful things is certainly different from walking and moving about, but it also has its benefits."

He took a sip from his mug and spoke quietly. "We are always going here, going there, doing this and doing that. Weather like this is Mother Nature's way of slowing us down. When snow falls and everything else is still except for our busy hands, that is the perfect time to relax our minds and to stop and appreciate all that we have. Nina used to love to make friendship bracelets. She would sit for hours working on one, making it perfect."

"Was Nina a friend?" Bobby asked.

"Yes!" he said smiling. "You could say that."

"Were those Nina's ice skates and snowshoes hanging on the wall in your store?" I asked.

"Yes," said Dave. "They are still full of Nina's young and happy spirit."

I pictured Nina in my mind, wearing her snowshoes as she hiked through the woods and skated on the nearby pond.

"Where is she now?" I asked.

"She is probably home, getting dinner started."

Bobby and I were confused.

Dave smiled. "When I was young I used to watch Nina from my window. One day, I decided to go outside and walk with her. A few years after that, I asked her to marry me. Nina is my wife."

"Are you Abenaki, too?" Bobby asked.

"Yes I am," replied Dave.

"DUDE that's so cool!" said Bobby.

"SUPER DUPER cool," smiled Dave.

Dave explained the meaning of the friendship bracelet to us. "They are called friendship bracelets because they are a continuous circle."

"When you have finished your last loop, you tie it onto the first loop. This forms a never-ending circle, which is what friendship is all about. But remember that beading is also a lesson in patience. You cannot be in a rush and you must go slowly in order to do it correctly."

Then he had to go. His wife Nina was making his favorite dinner, succotash* and rice.

❧ ❧

I thought about the meaning of the bracelets. My friends reminded me of the different colored beads, except, instead of different colors, they each had very different personalities.

As I wrapped the string of beads around my finger to form my next loop, I wished to myself that my friends could all fit together as nicely as the beads.

Chapter Seven
SLOW MAN

The next morning it had finally stopped snowing and the sun was shining bright. Bobby and I found some more snowshoes in the closet and decided to test them out in the snow.

We dressed warmly and then strapped on the snowshoes. Dad gave Bobby and me some ski poles for balance and off we went.

Dad, Bobby and I hiked a short distance into the woods. The snow-covered trees glistened in the sunlight. It was such a beautiful sight and it felt good to be outside. I felt like Nina, wandering through the woods, enjoying nature.

We came to a small clearing with breathtaking* views of the snowcapped peaks* far out in the distance. There were a few fallen logs near a stream that was rushing down the side of the mountain.

"This is the perfect place to stop for lunch," said Dad.

We sat on a log and Dad unpacked the sandwiches from his backpack.

It was the best picnic ever! Everything was so peaceful and I enjoyed listening to the trickling sounds coming from the nearby brook.

Then, all of a sudden, I heard a strange noise. AARRRP! It sounded like a bear. I jumped up and looked around nervously.

Dad and Bobby began to laugh hysterically.

"JUMPIN' JUPITER and GOSHARUNI GEE!" said Bobby. "You look like you've seen an alien."

"It was just Bobby burping," explained Dad.

I shouted at Bobby, "You scared the heck out of me! I thought we were being attacked by a bear!"

So much for enjoying the beautiful land-scape, I thought to myself, as I picked my lunch out of the snow.

Later that day, Bobby and I made a snow-man. Bobby called him the SLOW MAN because he came from the snow that made us go slow. We put a baseball cap on his head and then made a flag for him to hold. He looked just like the yellow plastic man that we some-times placed at the end of our driveway to warn drivers to go slowly.

"Now the cars won't go fast down this road and the moose will be really happy," said Bobby.

"Yeah," I joked, "like we really need to worry about that!"

ॐ ॐ

That evening, I worked some more on my bracelet. All that running around in the snow had tired Bobby out. He was already

upstairs, sound asleep.

As I sat there, working quietly, I realized that Dave was right. It was nice being still sometimes. And even though I missed my skating competition, I actually enjoyed being there, in the cabin, listening to the crackling sounds of the fireplace and working on my friendship bracelet.

That night I dreamed I was a young Abenaki girl, wandering the land. My snowshoes were very big and, as a result, I was having difficulty climbing up a mountain. I decided to rest on a log at the foot of the mountain and soon, I fell fast asleep.

When I awoke, there was a bear hovering* over me. He began shaking me. I tried to scream "Help me!" but no sound would come out of my mouth.

I tried to scream again, still no sound.

Chapter Eight
I'LL MOOSE YOU

"Wake up Katelyn. I have some GRRRREAT news! Wake up!" shouted Bobby.

I was a little confused at first and then I realized that it was only Bobby trying to shake me awake. I was so happy that he wasn't a bear.

"Katelyn," he shouted, "I have some BEARY GOOD NEWS! BEARY, BEARY GOOD NEWS! Look outside, just look!"

I climbed out of bed and walked over to the window. A man in a snowplow was motoring* down the mountain, clearing a path in the road.

"He's going way fast," said Bobby. "I need to have a talk with that SLOW MAN."

I ran downstairs. Bobby trailed behind

me. My mother was hanging up the telephone.

"The phones are working and I just spoke with Mrs. Billings," she said. "Your competition was postponed* on account of the weather. It's today. Everyone arrived last night. I explained to Mrs. Billings that we've been snowed in and that we would try to get you there in time."

"This MOOSE be your lucky day Katelyn!" smiled Bobby.

"If we leave soon, we just might make it," said my dad.

So we gathered up all of our things, packed up the car and were off!

ᑌᕼ ᑕᕼ

We drove down the mountain and made a quick stop at the general store to say goodbye to Dave.

I gave Dave a friendship bracelet that I made for him and thanked him for everything.

"I will nickname you Wandering Deer," said Dave, "because you are graceful like a deer and you have a lot of the same qualities that my wife Nina had when she was young."

"What about me?" asked Bobby. "Don't I get a nickname?"

"Oh yes," he answered. "I'm going to call you Red Squirrel. Busy mind, active spirit, always up to something—that's you!"

Bobby was pleased.

We said our goodbyes.

"ADIO!" said Dave. "That is how the Abenakis say goodbye today."

"LATER GATOR!" said Bobby.

"And *that*," I said, "is how pesky* little brothers say goodbye!"

❧ ❧

As we drove down Moose Mountain I thought about how much I was going to miss being there.

Bobby rolled down the car window. His voice echoed through the mountainside as he shouted his goodbyes. "GOODBYE LOG CABIN. GOODBYE MOOSE, I'LL MOOSE YOU! GOODBYE SYRUP LADY. GOODBYE NELLIE. GOODBYE SLOW MAN. GOOD-BYE SNOW. ADIO!"

Hello skating competition, I thought excitedly. I hoped that we would get there in time.

Chapter Nine
NERVOUS NELLIES

We were an hour late by the time we finally arrived at the skating arena. I grabbed my skating bag and rushed inside. I could hear the music playing as I hurried down the hallway to the rink. It was the music to "Somewhere Over the Rainbow." That was Annie's song! I began to run.

I got to the ice, and there was Annie moving and circling about with such grace. She looked so beautiful in her white velvet costume. She was wearing her hair in braids. I wondered what Mrs. Billings thought about that.

I watched her as she twirled and glided. I knew her routine by heart and I knew that her big axel jump was coming up. I held my breath as she readied herself.

She jumped up in the air and twirled and then landed perfectly. She nailed it! I let out a big sigh and then clapped along with the crowd. I was so proud of her and I was proud to be her friend.

She finished with a big bow and then skated off the ice. I rushed over to greet her.

"Annie!" I yelled, as she stepped off the ice.

"Katelyn!" She shouted.

We gave each other a big hug.

"I'm so glad you made it," said Annie.

"You were great out there and you skated perfectly," I told her.

Mrs. Billings was standing behind us. "Nice job Annie," she said.

Then she turned her attention to me. "Katelyn, you are already signed in. You go on in an hour so you need to be dressed and ready. Your warm-ups are in forty-five minutes."

"I'll be ready," I assured Mrs. Billings.

Annie's mom brought over a big bouquet of pink roses. She handed them to Annie and gave her a hug. Mrs. Billings told Annie that the scores for her group would be posted in a few minutes. We walked over to the sitting area to wait for the scores.

I told Annie all about our adventure in the mountains and explained how we had been snowbound for a few days. "That reminds me," I said, "I have something for you." I pulled the friendship bracelet that I made for Annie out of my coat pocket and handed it to her.

Annie smiled. "It's beautiful," she said. "It looks like you spent a lot of time on it."

"I had a lot of time to spend," I said.

I explained how each of the beads had different meanings and how the bracelet formed a never-ending circle symbolizing* friendship. "I wanted to give it to you for luck before you skated, but you really didn't need it," I said.

"I like it because it is a reminder of how nice you are to me," smiled Annie.

The scores were finally posted. Annie came in first place in her group. She was happy. We were all so proud of her.

A woman brought over a first-place medal and placed it around Annie's neck. We walked over to the photo area and Annie had her picture taken with the second- and third-place skaters.

Then we hurried into the locker room so that I could get ready.

I dressed quickly and Annie took out a bag of stuff to do my hair and makeup.

A few girls from another skating club entered the locker room. I did a double take when I saw what one of them was wearing. It was the glittery red costume from the catalog. The same exact one that I had wanted. Annie noticed, too. We both smiled at one another.

The girls from the other skating club were

a little loud and didn't seem to want to have much to do with us. The girl in the red costume walked over to the mirror and adjusted her out-fit. She stood there posing and admiring herself for quite some time.

We sat on a bench. Annie took out a brush and some bobby pins. I grabbed a mirror out of the bag and began applying my makeup.

"How did you get Mrs. Billings to agree to let you wear your hair in braids?" I asked.

"She changed her mind," said Annie. "I wore my hair in braids to the competition and when she saw me in my costume with my hair in braids she told me to keep it that way."

"I wonder what she would say if I wore my hair in a ponytail?" I thought out loud.

Annie started brushing my hair. "Do you want to try it and see how it looks?" she asked me.

"You know, it doesn't really matter to me now," I said. "I'm just so happy to be here. A bun will be just fine."

The girl in the red costume walked by and glanced down at us. I tried to smile at her but I just couldn't seem to make my mouth curve upwards. Instead, I think that my mouth made more of a frightened look. She smirked as she passed. I wasn't sure what to make of her.

"She reminds me of a woman who used to work at my father's company," said Annie. "You always knew when she was in a room with you because she talked really loud. It was as if she wanted to make sure that everyone noticed her."

"What does your dad do?" I asked Annie. "I heard he was a farmer."

"Well, sort of," answered Annie. "He owns a corn farm and now he has a canning business where he cans the corn and sells it across the country. He just opened a new canning facility and that's why we had to move. Have you ever heard of Hill's Corn?"

"Yes," I said. "My mom buys it all the time. Wow! So your dad is kind of like a big shot."

"Yeah, but you would never know it by speaking to him. To me, he's just my dad," said Annie.

I looked down at Annie's old skates. "Annie," I asked her, "why do you wear those skates? I mean..."

I was stumbling for the nicest way to tell her that her skates were a little worn and unattractive, when she interrupted me.

"These skates are my most favorite skates. My mom keeps bugging me to break in a new pair but I love the way these feel. And I can skate really well in them. So as long as they still fit me, I plan on wearing them."

Annie seemed to be able to read my thoughts. "At my old school, everyone pretty much wore jeans or overalls and a shirt. Nothing special, but that's how we liked it. No one cared much about dressing in the latest fads. My mom said that in some ways, moving to a different town and different state is almost like moving to a different country."

Mrs. Billings poked her head inside the locker room. "Time for warm-ups Katelyn."

Annie stuck the last bobby pin in my hair. I checked my lipstick in the mirror and then I added a little more blush, just because.

We walked out to the ice rink. I took off my skate guards. My mom, my dad and Bobby met us near the entrance to the ice.

"Good luck," said my mom.

My dad hugged me and whispered in my ear, "You'll do just great."

Bobby squeezed in between us. "BREAK A LEG!" he said. "That means good luck you know."

"Yes, I know," I answered.

"Oh, wait," continued Bobby, "I have something for you. I didn't spend much time on it because I'm a squirrel, you know. And squirrels are not very good at being still." He handed me the friendship bracelet that he had made. But it was very small, more like a friendship *ring*.

I placed it on my index finger where it fit just right.

"Even though you're my annoying *big* sister, you're still my friend," he said. "Sorta...kinda...you know what I mean."

I did. I knew just what he meant. I gave him a big hug and thanked him.

"And besides," he said, "if I gave it to my friend Sean, he would probably clock me!"

Annie crossed her fingers on both hands and held them up. That was our sign for good luck. I did the same.

I was competing against four other girls in

my group. We all skated out onto the ice for our ten minutes of warm-up time. The girl in the red costume kept skating around me. She shot me a look as she passed me on the ice. She was making me nervous and I felt as though she was trying to do it on purpose.

When the ten minutes were up, we all skated off the ice and waited for our turns to go on. The girl in red was first. I was after her.

The girl in red skated to a flashy* tango* routine. She moved quickly as she danced and skated around the ice. The decorative fringe on her costume seemed to be doing a dance all of its own.

When it came time for her to do her axel, she didn't land properly and she fell flat on her behind. She kept on smiling though, as she picked herself back up and carried on with her performance.

Finally, it was my turn. I skated out to the center of the ice and then waited for the music to begin. I could feel my heart pounding inside my chest and I kept reminding myself to breathe.

I swayed and glided to the music. I tried my hardest to smile and keep my chin up the entire time.

I knew my routine by heart and it was a good thing because I was too nervous to even think straight. As I stretched my arms out in front of me, I noticed the friendship ring that Bobby had given me. I laughed inside. Seeing the ring seemed to put everything in perspective*. This competition meant a lot to me, but not as much as my family and friends meant.

When it came time for my toe loop I executed it perfectly. I knew my axel jump was coming up next and I wasn't sure if I could do it. My foot slipped a little as I set up for the jump. I jumped up in the air and came down perfectly. Everyone clapped and I could hear Bobby shouting, "GRRRREAT job Katelyn!"

After my performance, I met everyone over by the sitting area. We had to wait for the rest of my group to finish before the scores were posted. Mrs. Billings told Annie and me that she was happy to see that all our hard work had paid off. Mom and Dad gave me a beautiful bouquet of red roses.

Annie and I paced back and forth. "You two are like a bunch of NERVOUS NELLIES!" joked Bobby. "Like two PEAS IN A POD. Like FRICK and FRACK!"

The girl with the red costume entered. Her face was red and swollen from crying.

"What's with Big Red?" asked Bobby.

"Big Red?" I asked.

"Yeah. That's what I call her," said Bobby. "She acts like a big shot and she's wearing that awful red costume, so I nicknamed her Big Red."

"I think she's upset because she fell," I answered.

"Big Red didn't do such a bad job," said Bobby. "She only fell that once. Other than that, I thought she was fun to watch."

❧ ❧

At last the scores were posted. Another girl in my group came in first place. I received a medal for second place and Big Red came in third. Finally! A medal. I was thrilled. We all posed for a picture in the photo area.

Afterward, Annie and I had our picture taken together. We held up our medals and smiled for the camera.

Then it was time to go home. Annie asked me if I wanted to come over to her house for dinner that Sunday, before we went

back to school. I said yes. I couldn't wait to meet the rest of her family and see her pet, Spike, that wasn't really a porcupine but a kitten that happened to look like one.

On the car ride home I told Mom, Dad and Bobby all about Annie's family and how her dad owned Hill's Corn.

"Pretty CORNY," said Bobby. "Pretty CORNY INDEED!"

Some things never change, I thought to myself.

Chapter Ten
STILL A STICKY SITUATION

That Sunday, I went over to Annie's house. I got to meet her dad, who didn't look at all like the farmer I had pictured, and her two older sisters, Molly and Madeline. We hung

out, listened to music and played with her pet, Spike. Spike was a cute kitten that really did look like a porcupine.

His gray fur stuck straight out all over his body and he had a tiny face with a little black spot on his nose. He was the most adorable kitty I had ever seen!

Annie's bedroom was the coolest. It was a garden theme with plants and flowers painted on the walls. There were flowerpots, a bag of dirt and seeds spread out on the table near her desk.

"What is all this?" I asked.

"Oh, that's for the science fair," she replied. " I'm really into science and I love anything to do with nature. My dad thought that I should do a project for the science fair. It's coming up in a few weeks, but I can't decide what to do." She paused for a moment. "Hey, do you want to do it with me?"

"Sure!" I said.

After brainstorming for a while, we finally decided to do an experiment to see how well corn seeds would grow if we fed them maple syrup instead of plant food.

"I have lots of maple syrup at my house," I told Annie. "I'll call my mom and ask her to bring us some when she comes to pick me up."

We placed soil in two pots and then sprinkled the seeds into each of them. We put plant food in one of the pots and labeled it as the control pot. The control pot holds the plant

that is grown in the traditional way, with water and plant food. Then we labeled the other pot as the test pot. This was the pot that we would add the maple syrup to.

Mom and Bobby came to pick me up. Bobby brought in the maple syrup. We poured the syrup into the soil of the test pot and then added water to both pots.

"There," said Annie, "now we just have to water them every couple of days, add more syrup to the test pot, and see what happens."

We said goodbye to Annie and I thanked her family for having me over to visit.

"See you tomorrow!" said Annie.

I climbed into the car and waved goodbye.

All of a sudden, I noticed that my hands were all gooey and sticky. I looked around. There was sticky stuff all over the door handle and the seat. "Why is it so sticky in here?" I asked.

"Oops," said Bobby, "I forgot to warn you. On the ride over I found a waffle in my pocket so I decided to put some syrup on it. But then Mom went over a *huge* bump and the syrup sorta spilled a little."

"A little? It's one big, sticky mess!" I complained as I tried to wipe my hands on my jeans.

Speaking of sticky...I was suddenly reminded of the other sticky situation that I still needed to deal with at school the next day.

Chapter Eleven
CHOOSING TO CHOOSE

It all came to a head in the school cafeteria. As I made my way from the lunch line, I noticed Annie, sitting by herself at a table. She looked up and smiled. I started to walk toward her when Caroline, Casey and Sarah began waving and yelling for me to sit with them.

And that's when it hit me! It all comes down to choices. Some choices are not ours to make, like when Mrs. Billings chose the lilac costume even though I really wanted the glittery red one. And when my parents decided to take a vacation before my competition even though I wanted to stay home and practice. Those were not choices that I wanted made for me.

Some choices are up to nature. We definitely cannot choose the weather. We can't ask the weather to wait a week before it dumps a huge pile of snow on our cabin, making it impossible for us to go anywhere!

Sometimes it's good that we can't choose because we're still young and we're still learning. If it were my decision, I would have tried to drive in the snowstorm so that I wouldn't miss my skating competition—probably not a good idea!

As I stood there in the school cafeteria, I realized that *I needed to choose*. This was one decision that I did have control over and… "GOSHARUNI GEE!" I wasn't going to make the wrong decision.

I felt my entire body shaking from nervousness as I walked over to Caroline, Casey and Sarah. It was the same exact feeling that I had when I was skating at the competition except this wasn't nearly as much fun.

"Hi guys," I said.

"Hi Katelyn," said Caroline. "Have a seat."

"Uh, that's OK," I said, "I'm going to sit with Annie today."

Caroline's mouth dropped. Casey was speechless for once and Sarah seemed really frightened for me.

"You're welcome to join us," I told them. They didn't know what to say, so I said good-bye and walked away.

I walked over to Annie's table and sat down beside her. Annie was happy to see me. We had a nice lunch together. We talked about skating and about the science fair. I was really curious to see how well the plant with the maple syrup would grow.

A little while later, Sarah came over to our table. Now it was my turn to be in shock. I had never known Sarah to do anything without Caroline's permission.

She stood there for a moment and then sat down beside Annie. "I decided that I needed to start deciding," said Sarah timidly*. She paused for a moment. "What I mean to say is that I need to start making my own decisions."

I was so pleased with Sarah for having the courage to make up her own mind.

For the next few days, things were a little awkward between Caroline, Casey, Sarah and me. Caroline wouldn't speak to Sarah or me. She passed us in the hallway without even saying hello.

Casey remained loyal to Caroline but gave me signs that she still liked me by smiling or waving to me in the lunch line when Caroline wasn't looking. Then one day I found an invitation to Caroline's birthday party in my school locker. Annie and Sarah each got one, too.

After school I called Caroline on the telephone. We talked small talk for a few minutes and then I broke the ice. I explained to her that making a choice to sit with Annie didn't mean that I didn't want to be her friend and that it was nice to have choices.

Caroline started to cry. She told me that she was afraid that if I became good friends with Annie I wouldn't want to hang out with her anymore.

"That's silly," I told her. "If I could take all of the things that I loved about all of my friends and combine them into one person then I wouldn't need any other friends. But that isn't how it works and I'm glad."

We made a pact. We decided that, from that point on, anyone would be welcome at our special table. And if one or two of us decided to sit with someone else at a different table, that would be OK, too.

Chapter Twelve
DON'T BUG ME!

It was the day of the science fair. The plant that was fed maple syrup didn't grow as well as the one without it.

Our pots and posters were set out nicely on our display table. Bobby wanted to hang around and help so we decided to let him.

He brought some small cups and handed out maple syrup samples to people. And when we weren't looking, Bobby stuck a bunch of gummy worms into the pots. He told us that the plants needed some color, particularly the one with the maple syrup.

Lots of people visited our table and we explained how our experiment worked. They seemed very interested. Bobby was convinced

that it was because of the free samples.

☙ ❧

Later that day, Mom took Bobby, Annie and me to the mall to run an errand. She let us each choose a treat at the candy store for doing such a good job on the science experiment.

"What should I get?" asked Annie. "There are so many choices."

I looked over at her. She had the prettiest

brown eyes and they were all lit up with excitement. "Well," I said, "I think that the chocolate-covered turtles are the best, but it's your choice. You choose!"

Bobby got his usual, sour gummy worms. I got the chocolate-covered turtles and Annie ended up choosing a piece of maple fudge. She was happy with her decision.

I was very happy with mine!

As we made our way through the mall we noticed that there was some sort of commotion* up ahead of us.

"Hey look, it's the maple syrup lady!" exclaimed Bobby.

It wasn't really the maple syrup lady. It was a giant poster of a ladybug. We walked over to where everyone was gathered. It appeared to be some sort of an exhibit, all about bugs.

The first table that we went to had a glass

cage filled with ladybugs. The cage was decorated with colorful plants and flowers and there were ladybugs everywhere. I watched them as they buzzed and wandered about. It was as if there were a hundred maple syrup ladies all in one place.

Bobby and Mom were already at the next table. Annie and I caught up with them. A woman was explaining how caterpillars turn into butterflies.

Bobby was fascinated with what she had

to say. He adored the fuzzy little creatures and was amazed to find out how they spin their own cocoons and then later, emerge* as beautiful butterflies.

There were some books for sale at the table that were all about caterpillars. Bobby reached in his pocket, pulled out his last few dollars and purchased a book. Mom was pleased to see that Bobby was using his allowance to buy a book instead of a toy.

⚜ ⚜

As we walked through the mall, Bobby could not take his head out of the book.

"Come on Bobby," I said, nudging him. "You're slowing us down."

"Stop BUGGING me Katelyn. I'm BZZZY looking at this book!" said Bobby.

"Hey Mom can I get a caterpillar?" asked Bobby. "I'll name him Creeper...actually, two caterpillars. I'll name one Jeepers and the other

Creepers because it's important that they each have a friend. I promise I'll take care of 'em."

He began rattling on and on about how much he really liked caterpillars and how interesting they were.

"Uh-oh," I said to my mom and Annie. "It looks like Bobby has found a new obsession."

We all laughed.

"Here we go again!"

Glossary

*Many words have more than one meaning. Here are the definitions of words marked with this symbol * (an asterisk) as they are used in sentences.*

annual: *yearly*
awkward: *uncomfortable, causing embarrassment*
axel: *in figure skating, a jump that begins from the outer forward edge of one skate, followed by one and one-half mid-air turns*
backward crossover: *passing the outside skate in front of the toe of the inside skate*
breathtaking: *beautiful, exciting*
chandelier: *lights that hang from the ceiling*
circumstances: *facts or events connected with a situation*
diameter: *the thickness or width of something*
clash: *to not match, or not go together*
commotion: *noise, action taking place*
competition: *a contest or challenge*

emerge: *appear or come into sight*

evaporated: *disappeared or changed into vapor*

fate: *chance or destiny*

fibbed: *lied, did not tell the truth*

fixated: *focused or concentrated on*

flashy: *fancy or showy*

ginormous: *enormous*

grungy: *ragged, worn out*

hauled: *moved, dragged or pulled*

hovering: *remaining near, floating above*

layback spin: *an upright spin, the arms are placed in a circle in front of the body and back is arched.*

motoring: *traveling or driving by car, auto or truck*

nor'easter: *a strong storm coming from the northeast*

notion: *idea, belief or opinion*

obsession: *an idea dominating one's thoughts*

peaks: *pointed tops of mountains or hills*

perspective: *understanding things or events*

pesky: *annoying, bothersome*
postponed: *put off until another time*
quirks: *unusual or odd habits*
ridiculous: *silly, foolish*
strutting: *walking or trotting confidently*
sturdy: *strong, well built*
succotash: *lima beans and corn cooked together*
symbolizing: *standing for something such as an idea or meaning*
tango: *Latin American music for dancing*
timber: *wood from trees*
timidly: *shyly, fearfully*
toe loop: *skater jumps into air from right back outside edge of skate with free leg rotation, does one rotation in the air*
traditional: *custom or beliefs handed down from the past; the way something is usually done*
vat: *a large tub or tank for holding liquids*
whined: *complained, moaned or sighed*

Daisy Chain Friendship Bracelet

Supplies:
1 bag of different colored seed beads (tiny beads)
Nylon bobbin thread
Size 10 or 12 beading needle
Beeswax

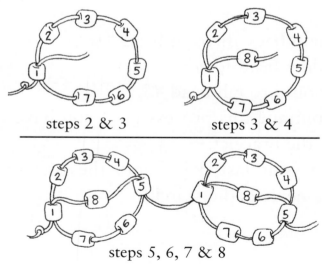

steps 2 & 3   steps 3 & 4

steps 5, 6, 7 & 8

1. Wax a piece of thread and then thread the needle. Pull one bead through and then tie it onto the end of the thread.

2. Add six more beads to make a total of seven beads for the flower.

3. Loop back through the first bead (#1) and then add a different color bead (#8) for the center of the flower.

4. Then loop through bead #5. This should form your first daisy.

5. Add seven more beads. You can choose a new color or stay with the same colors throughout.

6. Loop back through bead #1.

7. Add a bead for the center.

8. Loop through bead #5.

9. Continue this process until you have completed the bracelet.

10. Tie your last daisy onto the first one to form a never-ending circle.

Caution: The needles can be sharp. Depending on the age of the child, parents may need to assist with this project.

Tips: Pour some of the beads onto a plate. Then poke them with the needle to thread them through. Also, working on a table with the bracelet lying flat will help keep everything in place.

The colored beads have many meanings in the Native American culture. Some of these meanings are listed below:

Yellow (truth, growth, love)
Red (birth, clarity, new beginnings)
Black (lessons, adult, sunset)
White (purity, renewal, winter)
Blue (sky, water, spirit)
Green (earth, healing, health)